The Dome
And Minarets
Of A College
In Isfahan

IRAN

BY ELMA SCHEMENAUER

THE CHILD'S WORLD®, INC.

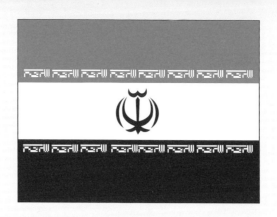

GRAPHIC DESIGN AND PRODUCTION
Robert E. Bonaker / Graphic Design & Consulting Co.

PHOTO RESEARCH
James R. Rothaus / James R. Rothaus & Associates

COVER PHOTO
Portrait of an Iranian girl
©Nazima Kowall/CORBIS

Library of Congress Cataloging-in-Publication Data
Schemenauer, Elma.
Iran / by Elma Schemenauer.
p. cm.
Includes index.
Summary: Briefly surveys the history, geography,
plants and animals, people, and culture of this
dry Middle Eastern country formerly called Persia.
ISBN 1-56766-738-4 (library reinforced : alk. paper)

1. Iran—Juvenile literature. [1. Iran.] I. Title.

DS254.75. S34 2000
955 — dc21   99-047488

Table
of
Contents

What if you were on a flying carpet soaring high above Earth? You would see huge land areas with water around them. These land areas are called **continents**. Some continents are made up of several countries. Iran is in the southwestern part of the continent of Asia.

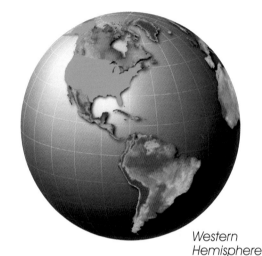

Western Hemisphere

Eastern Hemisphere

Iran (white) Is In The East And U.S.A. (green) Is In The West

Iran is an oil-rich country bordering the Gulf of Oman to the south and the Persian Gulf to the southwest. West of Iran is another oil-rich country, Iraq. North of Iran are the salty Caspian Sea and several countries, including Armenia and Turkmenistan. East of Iran are the countries of Afghanistan and Pakistan.

The World Shown Flat

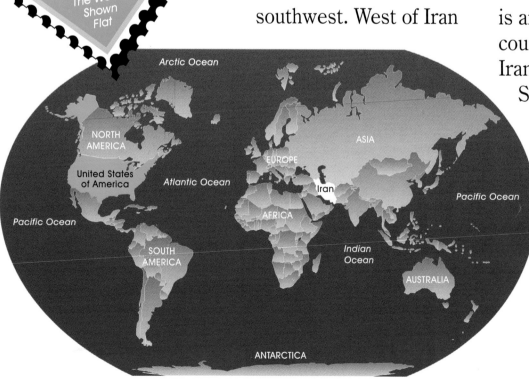

Arctic Ocean

NORTH AMERICA

United States of America

Atlantic Ocean

ASIA

EUROPE

Iran

Pacific Ocean

Pacific Ocean

AFRICA

SOUTH AMERICA

Indian Ocean

AUSTRALIA

ANTARCTICA

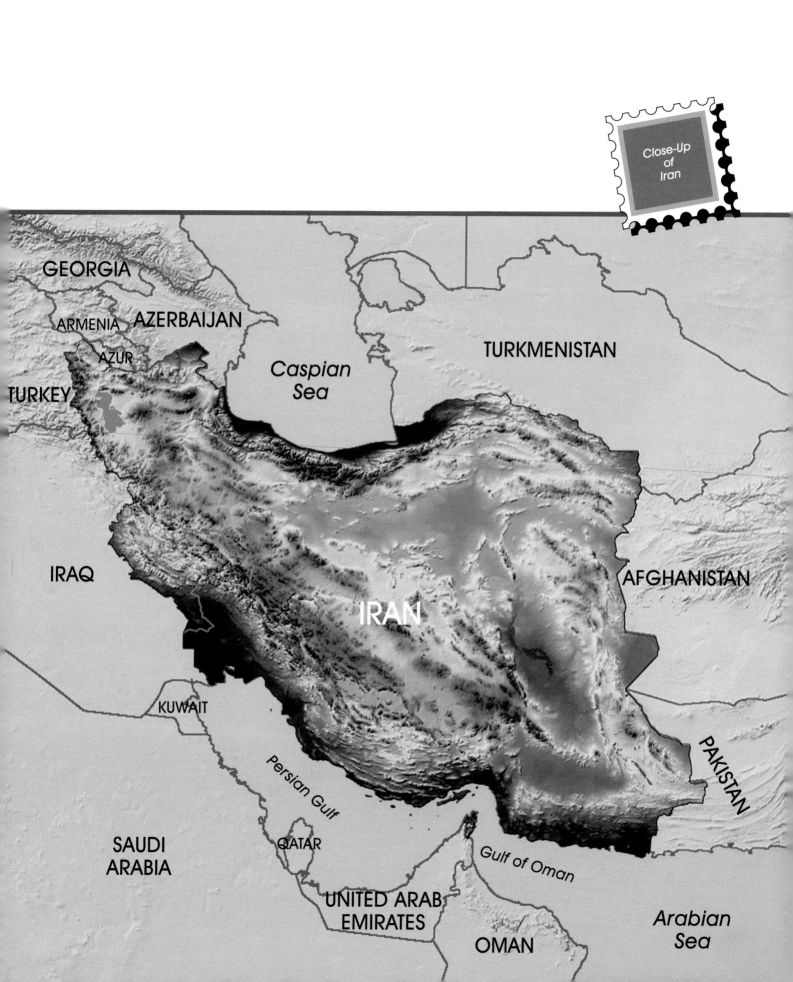

GEORGIA

ARMENIA   AZERBAIJAN

AZUR

TURKEY

Caspian Sea

TURKMENISTAN

IRAQ

IRAN

AFGHANISTAN

KUWAIT

PAKISTAN

Persian Gulf

SAUDI ARABIA

QATAR

Gulf of Oman

UNITED ARAB EMIRATES

OMAN

Arabian Sea

Iran's Only Volcano, Mount Damavand, Is The Tallest Mountain In Western Asia

+ MOUNT DAMAVAND

Isfahan
• Aga Gari

©CORBIS

A Fertile Valley In Northern Iran

©CORBIS

In the north, along the Caspian Sea, is a moist, green lowland that has Iran's richest soils. Many of its people live there. In the south and southwest, along the Gulf of Oman and Persian Gulf, is another lowland. Its southwestern end has some of Iran's richest oil fields.

A Desert Landscape Near Aga Gari

©Roger Wood/CORBIS

In the north and west are mountains. In Iran's middle and eastern parts is a high plain. Two deserts make up most of this plain. They are covered mostly by brown sand and gravel or by a crunchy crust of salt.

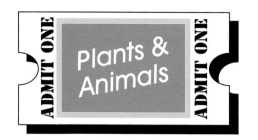

Plants & Animals

ADMIT ONE ADMIT ONE

Many of Iran's plants grow in the northern lowland and the mountains. Trees include elms, oaks, cypresses, and walnut trees. In the southern and southwestern lowland, date palms and other trees grow where they get enough water.

In the deserts, thorny shrubs struggle to live. Here and there across Iran are **oases**. Oases are areas watered by underground springs. In Iran's oases, grape vines, mulberry trees, willows, and poplars grow.

A Rice Field Near Bandar-e Anzali

©Brian Vikander/CORBIS

A Comb-Toed Gecko From Northern Iran

©David A. Northcott/CORBIS

Iran's animals include bears, wild sheep and goats, gazelles, and foxes. Birds include storks, falcons, pheasants, and partridges. Lizards skitter across the dry deserts.

©Earl & Nazima Kowall/CORBIS

Bandar-e Anzali

★Tehran

Trees
Line A Street
In Tehran

Ruins Of The
Ancient
Persian
Capital City
Of Persepolis

∴ PERSEPOLIS

A Painting Of A Finely Dressed Persian Woman

The earliest people in what is now Iran were hunters, farmers, and traders. About 3,000 years ago, iron-working Indo-Europeans came from what is now Russia. They formed two main tribes, the *Medes* and the *Persians*. About 500 years later, the Persians were ruling the Medes—and taking over other lands, too! The Persians were building a great Empire, but that ended in the year 642, when Arabs invaded Persia. The Arabs converted many of the people to the religion of **Islam**. More invaders came and went, but the country stayed Islamic.

In the early 1900s, oil was found in the area. Starting in 1925, Reza Shah Pahlavi, the king, used money from oil to build highways, factories, and seaports. He brought in Western (European and American) ideas and clothes. In 1935 he changed Persia's name to Iran, which means "Indo-European land," or "Aryan land."

A 19th Century Religious Ceremony

In 1941 Reza Shah's son became the king, or **shah**. Like his father, he brought many changes to Iran. But many Iranians didn't like him, so in 1979 he was forced leave. Islamic religious leader Ayatollah Khomeini took over, and the Islamic Revolution began. Western ideas and clothes were thrown out. Women had to wear head coverings and dresses down to their toes. Everyone was supposed to obey the laws of a strict kind of Islam. In 1989, Ayatollah Khomeini died. The new Ayatollah, Khamenei, kept on much the same way.

In 1997, Mohammed Khatami was elected president. He believes Iranians can have more freedom and still be good followers of Islam. Ayatollah Khamenei doesn't agree with all of Khatami's ideas. Some Iranians support Khatami and some support Khamenei.

Iranians Pulling Down A Statue Of Reza Shah Pahlavi In Tehran In 1979

©Bettmann/CORBIS

Members Of The Iranian Parliament In Tehran

©AFP/CORBIS

★Tehran

©Bettmann/CORBIS

Crowds Greeting Ayatollah Khomeini In Tehran In 1979

Women
In
Traditional
Black
Clothing
In Yazd

★Tehran

• Yazd

An Iranian Man Wearing A Turban In Yazd

©Earl & Nazima Kowall/CORBIS

The largest number of Iranians are Indo-Europeans like those who arrived long ago. Most of the Indo-Europeans are Persians, who often live in cities or settled farming areas. Among Iran's other Indo-Europeans are Kurds, Lurs, and Bakhtiari. Some of these people are **nomads**, moving from place to place to find food and water for their animals.

©Peter Turnley/CORBIS

An Iranian Family On A Motorcycle In Tehran

Many Iranians are related to the people of Turkey. They include Turkomans and Azerbaijanis. Iran also has small numbers of other people, including Arabs, Assyrians, and Armenians.

ADMIT ONE

City Life
And
Country
Life

ADMIT ONE

In cities, many Iranians live in brick or cement houses or apartments. Since many areas seldom get rain, roofs are often flat. People use them as breezy places to talk, play games, and relax. Inside, Iranians often sit not on chairs but on cozy carpets patterned in red, gold, black, and other colors. Families may serve their meals on carpets as well.

A Village On The Side Of A Cliff In The Alborz Mountain Range

©Brian Vikander/CORBIS

A Busy Street In Mashad

©Brian Vikander/CORBIS

In country villages where people live all year, many houses are much like those in cities. A number of country people, however, are nomads. Since they move around to find grassland for their sheep, goats, and other animals, many live in tents made of felt or other materials.

©Paul Almasy/CORBIS

ALBORZ MOUNTAINS

• Mashad

• Sultanasbad

Nomads
On The
Road To
Sultanasbad

A Nomadic School In The Country

★Tehran

Boys In Class In Tehran

©Peter Turnley/CORBIS

Many Iranian children start school at age six. Most schools stay in one place, but schools for nomads move right along with the nomads. Boys and girls attend separate classes. The most important thing they study is their religion, Islam. Its holy book, the **Quran,** is written in Arabic.

Arabic Writing In A Religious Manuscript

©CORBIS

Iran's official language, however, is Persian, or *Farsi*. It is related to the languages of India and Europe, including English. Persian uses the Arabic alphabet plus four extra letters. Persian, unlike English, is written from right to left.

©Roger Wood/CORBIS

Many Iranians pump oil out of the ground, **refine** it, and use it to make goods such as plastics, detergents, and jet fuel. Others work with natural gas. Some mine iron or copper, or collect desert salt to sell. Some work in factories making TV sets, washing machines, engines, shoes, and cloth. Iranian hand weavers make Persian carpets, which are famous around the world.

Farmers Harvesting Wheat Near Ahvaz

Farmers grow pistachios, almonds, wheat, rice, tea, fruit, and sugar beets. Among the animals raised are sheep, goats, cattle, water buffalo, chickens, and camels. Some Iranians fish for salmon and sturgeon.

©Earl & Nazima Kowall/CORBIS

An Iranian Carpet Weaver In Yazd

Ahvaz • Abadan • Yazd

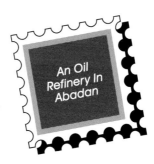

An Oil Refinery In Abadan

A Waiter Serving Tea To Customers In A Restaurant In Tehran

• Khavin

★Tehran

• Bishapur

©Earl & Nazima Kowall/CORBIS

A Woman Making Bread Near Bishapur

©Earl & Nazima Kowall/CORBIS

Rice, grown in the moist Caspian Sea lowland, is one of Iran's most important foods. People eat it with chicken, fish, beef, carrots, lentils, or beans. Fresh hot bread is also important. For breakfast people often eat bread with cheese, honey, or **halvah,** made from honey and ground sesame seeds.

A Man Selling Vegetables At The Khavin Market

©Roger Wood/CORBIS

Iranians enjoy yogurt. They eat it by itself or in a soup with barley and onions. They also use yogurt to flavor lamb for their national dish, lamb kebabs with rice. Some of the fruits Iranians grow and eat are dates, oranges, grapes, apples, and Persian melons. Tea is their favorite drink. It is against the Islamic religion to drink wine or other alcoholic drinks, or to eat pork.

Skiing in the mountains, swimming, soccer, horse racing, weight lifting, and wrestling are favorite sports in Iran. Iranians invented **polo**, a sport played on horseback, and they still enjoy it. Another sport is a mix of wrestling and gymnastics. Found almost nowhere else in the world, it takes place in Iranian clubs called *zurkhanehs*.

Among games Iranians enjoy are backgammon and chess. They also watch TV and films. Iranian filmmakers are known for making good films. But they must be careful, since everything shown on screen in Iran is supposed to follow strict Islamic rules.

In Iran the weekend holiday is Friday (not Saturday or Sunday). For many Iranians, an important yearly holiday is *No Ruz*, or New Year's. Other holidays are the prophet Mohammed's birthday and **Ramadan**, a month of daytime fasting. On February 11 Iranians celebrate the Magnificent Victory of the Islamic Revolution of Iran. On that day they remember Ayatollah Khomeini's takeover of the government in 1979.

Outsiders often have a hard time understanding Iran. Today the country faces new challenges. Some Iranian leaders want to stay with Khamenei's strict governing style. Others want more freedom for women and for people with different political ideas. It will be interesting to see what happens.

A Family Celebrating The New Year In Tehran

©Paul Almasy/CORBIS

★Tehran

• Shiraz

Men Exercising At The Jaffary Zurkhaneh In Tehran

Area
About 636,000 square miles (1.6 million square kilometers)—a bit bigger than Alaska.

Population
More than 71 million people.

Capital City
Tehran.

Other Important Cities
Mashhad, Isfahan, Tabriz, and Shiraz.

Money
The rial.

National Flag
The flag has three sideways stripes of green, white, and red. On the inside edges of the green and red stripes are the words *Allah Akbar* (God is great). In red, in the middle of the white stripe, is Iran's coat of arms.

National Dish
Lamb kebabs with rice.

National Language
Persian.

National Holiday
Islamic Republic Day on April 1.

Heads of Government
The Faqih of Iran (national religious leader) and the president of Iran.

Islamic Tilework At A Museum In Shiraz

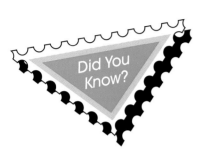

Did You Know?

Iran is really called "The Islamic Republic of Iran." People often just say "Iran" for short.

Iran is one of the world's oldest countries. The Bible mentions some of its leaders, such as Cyrus, who was the king of Persia.

Pistachio trees first grew in Iran, which still leads the world in growing pistachio nuts.

In the countryside, Iranian children often help their families by watching flocks of sheep or goats.

How Do You Say?

	PERSIAN, OR FARSI	HOW TO SAY IT
Hello	sal m	sah–LAHM
Good-bye	khod h fez	koh–DAH ha–FEZ
Please	lotfan	lot–FAN
Thank You	mamnoon am	mam–NOON am
One	yek	YEK
Two	do	DOH
Three	seh	SEH
Iran	Iran	ee–RRAN

continents (KON–tih–nents)
Most of Earth's land areas are in huge sections called continents. Iran is located on the continent of Asia.

halvah (HAL–vuh)
Halvah is a sweet paste made with sesame seeds and honey. Many Iranians eat bread with halvah for breakfast.

Islam (IS–lam)
Islam is a set of beliefs about God (called Allah) and his prophet Muhammad. Many people in Saudi Arabia belong to the Islamic faith.

nomads (NOH–madz)
Nomads are people who move from place to place rather than living in one home. Some Iranians are nomads.

oases (oh-AY–seez)
Oases are places in the desert that get water from underground springs. Most oases have green plants and trees.

polo (POH–loh)
Polo is a game where players ride on horses and try to hit a ball with a mallet. Polo is a popular sport in Iran.

Quran (koo-RRAHN)
The Quran is the holy book of the religion of Islam. Many Iranians follow the Islamic faith.

Ramadan (RAH–muh–dahn)
Ramadan is an Islamic religious holiday. During Ramadan, people do not eat between sunrise and sunset.

refine (ree–FINE)
When you refine something, you get rid of the parts you don't want. Many Iranians refine oil to make fuels and other products.

shah (SHAH)
Iran's king was called a shah. In 1979, the Shah of Iran was replaced by Ayatollah Khomeini.

Index

Web Sites

Learn more about Iran!

Visit our homepage for lots of links about Iran:

http://www.childsworld.com/links.html

Note to Parents, Teachers, and Librarians:
We routinely verify our Web links to make sure they're safe,
active sites—so encourage your readers to check them out!